The Fort

Laura Perdew

illustrated by **Adelina Lirius**

PAGE
STREET
KIDS

As the prince strutted toward his castle,
he daydreamed about the royal feast he was planning.
He imagined music and food and fun with friends.

But when he crossed over the moat to begin
decorating, the prince discovered that the castle
was not at all like he'd left it.

"What's this? A useless treasure map scribbled on MY invitation!" The prince paced around the great hall and stepped on an eyepatch.

"Oh no! A pirate
has invaded my castle!"

The prince tidied up and rid the castle
of all things pirate.

He wasn't about to let a rotten pirate keep him
from hosting his royal feast.

The next day, as the pirate paraded toward
her ship, she daydreamed about the swashbuckling voyage
she was charting. She imagined overflowing treasure
chests and adventures on the high seas.

But when she walked up the gangway to ready
the ship, the pirate discovered that someone else
had been aboard.

"Aaarrrgggghhh! An invitation to a silly feast written on MY treasure map?" The pirate clomped around the galley and tripped on a crown.

"Shiver me timbers!
A prince has raided my ship!"

The pirate swabbed the decks and
rid the ship of all things royal.

She wasn't about to let a pompous prince keep her
from sailing away to find treasure.

The prince returned the next morning, only to find that once again his castle was not at all like he'd left it.

"That dreadful pirate has made a mess of everything!" he cried.

Late that afternoon, the pirate discovered that yet again someone had been aboard her ship.

"That puffed-up prince came back!" she bellowed.

When the prince arrived at his castle on the day of the royal feast, he yanked the tablecloth off the flagpole and smoothed it down on the tabletop. Then he heard a voice outside.

A pirate voice. Singing a sea chanty.

"Blow me down!" the pirate hollered.
"What are you doing on MY ship?"

"Nonsense! This is MY castle. And if you don't stay out,
I will put you in the dungeon!" declared the prince.

He stomped onto the drawbridge to defend the castle.

The pirate seized her sword from him to stop the mutiny.
**"Never! I will not abandon my ship! If you don't leave,
I'll make you walk the gangplank!"**

"You can't! I am planning a royal feast for friends."

The prince waved the invitation.

"No pirates allowed."

The pirate grabbed the paper.
"And I am going on an adventure in
search of buried treasure.
No royalty allowed."

"Who wants to live on a stinky ship anyway?" shouted the prince. "I'd rather go to the moon!"

They both eyed the fort.

"**Aye**," she said.
"**A voyage . . . into space?**"

"On a spaceship?" he asked,
imagining being the mission commander,
guiding their spacecraft, and orbiting Earth together.

"**Yes . . . on this spaceship**," she agreed,
imagining being the chief scientist, leading space exploration,
and making new scientific discoveries.

"**Close the hatch!**"

The two astronauts
prepared the spaceship for launch.
She inspected their space helmets.
He adjusted their oxygen hoses.

She tested the robotic arm.

He studied the mission instructions.

"Mission control, ready for departure."

"Ten,

nine,

eight,

seven,

six,

five,

four,

three,

two,

one!"

For children young and old—may you discover
the power of imagination and compromise,
and the magic of a fort.
— L. P.

To Martin, for the love and support.
— A. L.

Text copyright © 2020 Laura Perdew
Illustrations copyright © 2020 Adelina Lirius

First published in 2020 by Page Street Kids,
an imprint of
Page Street Publishing Co.
27 Congress Street, Suite 1511
Salem, MA 01970
www.pagestreetpublishing.com

22 23 24 CCO 5 4 3

ISBN-13: 978-1-62414-925-2. ISBN-10: 1-624-14925-1
CIP data for this book is available from the Library of Congress.

This book was typeset in Charcuterie Flared. The illustrations were done using mixed media.
Printed and bound in Shenzhen, Guangdong, China.

Page Street Publishing uses only materials from suppliers who are committed to responsible and sustainable forest management.
Page Street Publishing protects our planet by donating to nonprofits like The Trustees, which focuses on local land conservation.

trustees